# I Can Soar

## Darlene Hubbard-Williamson

### Illustrated by: Asim Wilson

# I CAN SOAR

Darlene Williamson

Library of Congress
©2010 by Darlene Williamson

ISBN 13:  978-0-9726109-1-9

Cover design: Matthew Williams, Sr.
Illustrations: Asim Wilson

# DEDICATION

This book is dedicated
to all children.

# ACKNOWLEDGEMENTS

I am grateful to God for looking beyond my faults and always seeing my needs. I am grateful to God for life, my parents, my sisters, my grandparents as well as my extended family. I am thankful to God for inspiring me to write this book.  It is truly a dream that came true.

I am thankful to God for the wonderful, growing partnership, and precious relationship that I share with my husband, Stacy Williamson. Stacy, thank you so much for your loving support and sacrifice.

I am thankful to God for my two children, Stacy and O'Shae. I am excited about your future. Mommy loves you so much.

I am thankful to God for all of my teachers and mentors. Special thanks to Rev. Dr. Lance D. Watson, Pastor of The Saint Paul's Baptist Church in Richmond, Virginia, who always inspires me to keep GROWING by the grace of God each day. Thanks to my co-laborers in the vineyard as well as our growing congregation at Saint Paul's Baptist Church. Thank you for your support and prayers St. Paul's.

I am thankful to God for Asim Wilson for the incredible work in such a short time. I am truly amazed by the way you captured the vision for "I Can Soar."

There was a colorful bird named Jessie.
Jessie was a very timid bird.

Jessie enjoyed making friends and helping others.

Jessie became very discouraged because she could not soar in the sky like the other colorful birds. Jessie was very afraid that the hungry predators that were lurking around below would capture her.

One evening, while Jessie was playing with her friends, one of the hungry predators caught her by her wings.

The predator and his family took her and put her in a cage. They later decided to eat Jessie for dinner. Meanwhile the predators were thinking of ways to cook her.

While the predators were searching for a recipe, their eyes were pierced in the cookbook and they took their eyes off of Jessie.

Jessie remembered that they forgot to put the latch on the door of the cage. Therefore, Jessie was able to escape out of the cage and through an open window.

Eventually, one of the predators saw Jessie escaping and they began to chase her.

But, up above Jessie, there was one of her friends and she caught her by the wings and soared in the sky out of reach of the predators.

Jessie's family and friends were concerned about Jessie's condition. After all, colorful birds were known to soar in the sky.

The other colorful birds were afraid that the hungry predators would capture Jessie again. Therefore, they suggested that Jessie visit the doctor.

One day Jessie decided to visit Dr. Stacy O'Shae, so she could soar in the sky like the rest of the colorful birds.

Jessie could barely fly into the doctor's office. While Dr. Stacy O'Shae was waiting on another patient, Jessie waited patiently for her turn for help.

Finally, it was Jessie's turn to see the doctor. Instantly, without Jessie speaking, the doctor knew what Jessie needed.

The doctor stretched Jessie's wings outward in a praised position and raised Jessie's beak toward heaven. The doctor replied, "Awww, you've been flying low for so long that you forgot how to soar."

As the other birds watched and cheered, Jessie flew out of the doctor's office soaring. Jessie flew so high in the sky that she was above every colorful bird in the entire sky.

## The Inspirational Message:

God created us to soar on wings like eagles. If you ever need any assistance, you can always call on "Doctor Jesus." He always knows what we need. The Bible says in Isaiah 40:31, "But those who trust in the Lord will find new strength. They will soar high on wings like eagles…"

# DARLENE HUBBARD-WILLIAMSON

Darlene Hubbard-Williamson is the daughter of the late Jessie Stephenson Hubbard and Donald Leigh Hubbard. She is married to Stacy Lamar Williamson. They have been married for 21 years and have two impressive sons, Minister Stacy Lamar Williamson, Jr. and O'Shae Javon Williamson.

www.ingramcontent.com/pod-product-compliance
Lightning Source LLC
Chambersburg PA
CBHW042137120726
47911CB00022B/108